ERIC CARLE
The Greedy Python

by Richard Buckley   illustrated by Eric Carle

READY-TO-READ

SIMON SPOTLIGHT
New York London Toronto Sydney New Delhi

SIMON SPOTLIGHT

An imprint of Simon & Schuster Children's Publishing Division

1230 Avenue of the Americas, New York, New York 10020

Originally published in the United States by Picture Book Studio 1985

First Simon Spotlight Ready-to-Read edition 2012

For information about special discounts for bulk purchases, please contact Simon & Schuster Special Sales at 1-866-506-1949 or business@simonandschuster.com.

The Simon & Schuster Speakers Bureau can bring authors to your live event. For more information or to book an event contact the Simon & Schuster Speakers Bureau at 1-866-248-3049 or visit our website at www.simonspeakers.com.

Manufactured in the United States of America 0312 LAK

First Edition

2 4 6 8 10 9 7 5 3 1

Library of Congress Cataloging-in-Publication Data

Buckley, Richard, 1938-

The greedy python / by Richard Buckley ; illustrated by Eric Carle. — 1st ed.

p. cm. — (Ready-to-read)

Summary: A greedy python eats to excess, finally eating himself.

ISBN 978-1-4424-4576-5 (pbk.) — ISBN 978-1-4424-4577-2 (hardcover)

[1. Stories in rhyme. 2. Greed—Fiction. 3. Pythons—Fiction. 4. Snakes—Fiction. 5. Food habits—Fiction.] I. Carle, Eric, ill. II. Title.

PZ8.3.B8474Gr 2012

[E]—dc23

2011025822

This book was previously published with slightly different text.

Half hidden
in the jungle green,
the biggest snake
that there has been
looped back and forth
and in between.

The giant snake was

very strong,

and very, very,
very long.

He had a big, huge appetite.
His belly stretched
from left to right.

He quickly gobbled
in one bite
all animals
that came in sight:

a mouse that hurried
to and fro,

a frog that jumped up
from below,

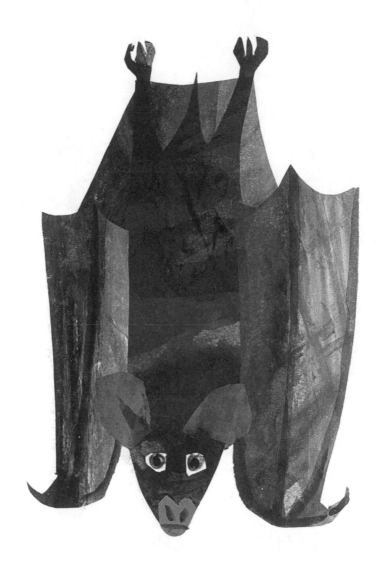

a bat that hung

from his left toe,

a fish that swam
a bit too slow,

a bird that flew a bit too low,

a porcupine
still half asleep,

a monkey who was

in mid-leap,

a leopard sitting in a tree,

a buffalo who came to see.

An elephant,
complete with trunk,
was swallowed
in a single chunk.
"I am too big
for you!"
he cried.

"No, you are not!"
the snake replied.

At last the python's meal
was done,
and he lay resting
in the sun.

The animals inside of him
began to jump and fly
and swim.

And when they all
began to kick,
the snake began
to feel quite sick.

He coughed the whole lot
up again.
Each one of them, and there
were ten.

He soon felt better.
What is more,
he was hungrier than before.
He had not learned
a single thing.

His greed was quite astonishing.

He saw his own tail,
long and curved,
and thought that lunch
was being served.

He closed his jaws

on his own rear,

then swallowed hard . . .

. . . and disappeared!